TITCHY WITCH

and the

Get-Better Spell

Rose Impey ★ Katharine McEwen

ORCHARD BOOKS

Titchy-witch

Victor

Eric

Wendel

Weeny-witch

Witchy-witch

Cat-a-bogus

For Beccy
R.I.

To Hannah and Jamie
K.M.

Orchard Books
96 Leonard Street, London EC2A 4XD
Orchard Books Australia
32/45-51 Huntley Street, Alexandria, NSW 2015
First published in Great Britain in 2003
First paperback publication 2004
ISBN 1 84121 052 8 (HB)
ISBN 1 84121 128 1 (PB)
Text © Rose Impey 2003 Illustrations © Katharine McEwen 2003
The rights of Rose Impey to be identified as the author and
Katharine McEwen to be identified as the illustrator of this Work
have been asserted by them in accordance with the
Copyright, Designs and Patents Act, 1988.
A CIP catalogue record for this book is available from the British Library
1 3 5 7 9 10 8 6 4 2 (HB)
1 3 5 7 9 10 8 6 4 2 (PB)
Printed in Hong Kong

Witchy-witch and the baby had witchy flu.
They did look poorly.

Wendel was away, on a wizard
weekend.
So Cat-a-bogus was in charge.
"Back to bed with you
two," he said.

"What about me?" said
Titchy-witch.
"You can stay out of trouble!"

Titchy-witch thought *she* would make a much better nurse than Cat-a-bogus.

She made a nice drink and
took it upstairs to Mum.

But Cat-a-bogus shooed her away.
"Out, out!" growled the cat. "Before
you catch the flu, too."

"I'll find you a job," he snapped.
Titchy-witch didn't like the sound
of that.

"We'll make a big pot of Get-Better Soup," said the Cat. "Just the thing to put a poorly witch back on her broomstick."

First he told Dido to peel a pile
of carrots.

Then he sent Titchy-witch out
to collect caterpillars.

"Soup!" grumbled Titchy-witch.
What good was soup?
Witchy-witch needed a Get-Better
spell.

And Titchy-witch was just the little witch to make it.

She put in lots of noisy things to
bring her mum's voice back:

"Croak of frog, bark of dog,
squeak of bat, purr of cat,
bees' hum…"

"Hmmm, too quiet!" she thought.
She needed something louder.

"bang of drum!"

But then Titchy-witch got a bit
excited.

"Thunder's crash! Lightning's flash!
Fireworks' bang! Hammers' clang!"

It was such a noisy spell, that
Titchy-witch had to hide it in her
hat while she took it upstairs.

But Cat-a-bogus was still
on the prowl.

She hid in the kitchen until he
had gone.
Mmmm! The soup was
smelling good.

Just then Dido started to hiss and rattle his tail. Cat-a-bogus was coming!

If the cat came in and found
her with the spell she was in
big trouble.
Quickly she threw it into the
pan of soup.

Glug! Glug! Gluga-lug!
Glop! Glop! Gloop!
The soup boiled and bubbled like
a volcano.

It was so noisy, Titchy-witch had to
make up a new spell, as fast as
she could:

"Parsley, basil, mint and dill,
Soup stop boiling, soup be still!"

The soup stopped bubbling and
simmered gently in the pan.

When Cat-a-bogus came in,
Titchy-witch looked as if maggots
wouldn't melt in her mouth.

Smells good

"Hmmm," purred the cat. "Smells even better than usual."

Mum and the baby were soon
feeling well.
Cat-a-bogus said that was because
of the Get-Better Soup.

But Titchy-witch and Dido knew better.

TITCHY WITCH

Rose Impey ★ Katharine McEwen

Enjoy a little more magic with all the Titchy-witch tales:

❏ Titchy-witch and the Birthday Broomstick   1 84121 120 6

❏ Titchy-witch and the Disappearing Baby   1 84121 116 8

❏ Titchy-witch and the Frog Fiasco   1 84121 122 2

❏ Titchy-witch and the Stray Dragon   1 84121 118 4

❏ Titchy-witch and the Bully-Boggarts   1 84121 124 9

❏ Titchy-witch and the Wobbly Fang   1 84121 126 5

❏ Titchy-witch and the Get-Better Spell   1 84121 128 1

❏ Titchy-witch and the Magic Party   1 84121 130 3

All priced at £4.99 each

Colour Crunchies are available from all good
bookshops, or can be ordered direct from the publisher:
Orchard Books, PO BOX 29, Douglas IM99 1BQ
Credit card orders please telephone 01624 836000
or fax 01624 837033
or e-mail: bookshop@enterprise.net for details.

To order please quote title, author and ISBN
and your full name and address.
Cheques and postal orders should be
made payable to 'Bookpost plc'.
Postage and packing is FREE within the UK
(overseas customers should add £1.00 per book).

Prices and availability are subject to change.